Kumba and Kambili

A TALE FROM MALI

Retold by Suzanne I. Barchers
Illustrated by Keith D. Shepherd

RED
CHAIR
•PRESS•

Please visit our website at **www.redchairpress.com**.
Find a free catalog of all our high-quality products for young readers.

For a free activity page for this story, go to
www.redchairpress.com and look for Free Activities.

Kumba and Kambili

Publisher's Cataloging-In-Publication Data
(Prepared by The Donohue Group, Inc.)

Barchers, Suzanne I.
Kumba and Kambili : a tale from Mali / retold by Suzanne I. Barchers ;
illustrated by Keith D. Shepherd.
p. : col. ill. ; cm. -- (Tales of honor)
Summary: When the village is terrorized by a lion, the hunter Kambili
wishes to track down the beast. However, his wife Kumba steps in to
warn him that the lion is actually an evil wizard. Together the brave
Kumba and Kambili prove no match for the lion-man. Includes special
educational sections: Words to know, What do you think?, and About Mali.
Interest age level: 006-010.
ISBN: 978-1-937529-74-1 (lib. binding/hardcover)
ISBN: 978-1-937529-58-1 (pbk.)
ISBN: 978-1-936163-90-8 (eBook)
1. Courage--Mali--Juvenile fiction. 2. Hunters--Mali--Juvenile fiction.
3. Lion--Mali--Juvenile fiction. 4. Mandingo (African people)--Folklore.
5. Folklore--Mali. 6. Courage--Mali--Fiction. 7. Hunters--Mali--Fiction.
8. Lions--Mali--Fiction. 9. Mandingo (African people)--Folklore.
10. Folklore--Mali. I. Shepherd, Keith D., 1957- II. Title.

PZ8.1.B37 Ku 2013

398.2/73/096623   2012951560

This series first published by:
Red Chair Press LLC   PO Box 333   South Egremont, MA 01258-0333

Printed in the United States of America

1 2 3 4 5 18 17 16 15 14

Each night when the sky turned dark, the Malinke people hid in their huts. Each night, a lion crept into the villages. Each night, the lion killed all those he caught.

The people turned to a brave man for help.
"Kambili, you are strong and bold. Please save us.
Find the lion and stop it!" the people begged.

Kambili answered, "We have all lost someone
we love. I will try, but I need to know more
about this lion."

The next day Kambili talked with his wife.
"Kumba, sing to the spirits. Find out what you
can about the lion. Where does it come from?
How can I stop it?"

Kumba sang. She listened to her heart.
Then she told Kambili what she had learned.

"This is not just a lion," Kumba said. "It is a powerful wizard that turns into a lion each night. The only way to stop him is to kill him."

Kambili looked at Kumba in dismay.
"A wizard? How can I kill a wizard? They have strong powers." Kumba said, "I have an idea. There is a clearing near the village of Jimini. We can lure him there. Then you can kill him."

Kambili thought for a minute and said,
"That might work. When hunters want to
catch a lion, they tie a goat to a tree as bait.
But this lion prefers the flesh of man to the
flesh of a goat."

Kumba said, "Then I will be the bait. We know
he comes at night. You can hide. Once it is
dark, I'll sing. He'll hear me and come to get
me. But then you can kill him."

Kambili cried, "It is too dangerous! I can't let you do that. I can't risk losing you Kumba."

"But you are the one at risk," Kumba replied. "You have to fight him. You will be in more danger."

Kambili thought for a moment. "I know it's a good plan. But what if I fail?"

Kumba replied, "You won't. And if you are bold enough to fight the beast, then I am brave enough to set the trap." Kambili smiled sadly at his wife. "All right. Let's leave now so we can be ready tonight."

Kumba and Kambili went to the grove. Kumba
leaned against a tree. Kambili hid in the
bushes. They watched the sky change from a
hazy blue to a blushing pink. Finally the soft
black of night was shadowed by the moon.

As the stars shimmered, Kumba began to
sing. The song drifted to where the lion-man
prowled. She sang so sweetly that the lion-man
knew he had to have her for his next meal.

As the beast crept to the grove, he filled the air with a spell of sleep. Kumba's singing kept her from getting sleepy. But Kambili could not resist. His eyes began to close. His head dropped to his chest. He was lost in sleep as a cloud drifted across the moon.

When the moonlight returned, the lion-man spotted Kumba. His eyes glowed with greed. Kumba sensed that the lion was near. She called softly, "Kambili...he's here. Kambili..."

Kumba kept singing. But Kambili did not come. She sang more loudly.

The lion crouched for his attack just as Kambili lifted his head. He was jolted awake by sight of the lion about to leap on Kumba.

Kambili bounded from the bushes. He landed between Kumba and the lion. He lifted his spear with a howl of rage.

The lion could not stop his leap. Kambili thrust
the spear into the lion's chest. The beast fell to
the ground with a thud.

Kumba and Kambili watched as the lion
changed back to the form of the wizard.
It was over. The lion-man was dead.

They walked wearily back to the village to share the news.

The villagers honored both Kumba and
Kambili for their bravery. Without his wise and
clever wife, the brave Kambili could not have
slain the dreaded beast.

bait: something used to tempt or entice other animals

dismay: concern or distress

dreaded: to be thought of with fear

Malinke: a group of people living mainly in Senegal, Mali, and Ivory Coast

wizard: in fairy tales and legends, a man with magical powers

WHAT DO YOU THINK?

Question 1: Why did the people of the village turn to Kambili to ask for help?

Question 2: Kumba agreed to be the one to attract the lion. Do you think she was afraid?

Question 3: This is a story about bravery and courage. Who do you think was more brave, Kumba or her husband Kambili? Why?

About Mali

The Republic of Mali in Western Africa has been part of three important empires that controlled trade across the Sahara for centuries. The great Mali Empire of the Malinke (or Mandinka) ruled millions of people in parts of present-day Guinea, Ivory Coast, Senegal, and Mali. It is believed Mali takes its name from these proud people. The Malinke today still pride themselves on the tradition of story-telling and proverbs.

About the Author

After fifteen years as a teacher, Suzanne Barchers began a career in writing and publishing. She has written over 100 children's books, two college textbooks, and more than 20 reader's theater and teacher resource books. She previously held editorial roles at Weekly Reader and LeapFrog and is on the PBS Kids Media Advisory Board. Suzanne also plays the flute professionally – and for fun – from her home in Stanford, CA.

About the Illustrator

Keith D. Shepherd is an educator, illustrator and painter. His works have been in galleries, museums and private collections across the U.S. Born in St. Louis, Keith now lives and works in Kansas City, Missouri.